To the stronger gender.

My grandmother, for introducing me to the world of stories. My teachers at Toc-H Public School, for giving me words. My daughters, for letting my imagination free. My mother, for always giving me the best. My best friend, for believing in me even when I did not.

- Sreedev

To my lovely darlings.

My family and friends who have supported me and will keep believing in me no matter what.

- Shilpa

From the creators

'Keep Gliding' is an attempt to revive our friendship from school. It's been more than 20 years since we left the walls of Toc-H Public School, Cochin, India where we had the best times.

Through Keep Gliding, we have experimented with a few short fictional narratives, held together by the theme that the frame of life is larger than what our eyes see. Through this work, we are supporting UNICEF in our small way.

Your reading this is a big success for us. Hope you enjoy it as much as we did while putting it together.

Many thanks

Shilpa and Sreedev

Big Hugs

Sandeep Balan, Shashikala Miss and Suma Miss.
Without your love, Keep Gliding would not have
come out the way it has.

Foreword

I have always found it fascinating how destiny manages to intertwine your paths with complete strangers in the most unexpected ways and they end up becoming an integral part of your life journey. And that's exactly how it has been with Sree, the author of this lovely book you are about to experience.

It took a chance meeting at a common friend's place, for me to get chatting with him. And to think that we spent all our student days holed up in our respective campuses, a stone's throw away, oblivious of each other's existence. For a Malayalee (someone who speaks the language Malayalam, the native language of Kerala, India), to find one of your brethren in a foreign land, is like finding oasis in a desert. So, it's surprising that despite being within a few hundred metres of each other for this long, our paths never crossed. And when it eventually did, we hit it off instantly.

Post a few brief catch ups that followed, our paths drifted again. Sree moved to pursue his professional aspirations in another geography and I was extremely lucky to be able to make the transition from writing short stories on my blog to writing for the screen. And I consider myself fortunate to have some of these stories being shared extensively over the internet as they went viral, finding its way to Sree eventually.

It was these stories that ensured that we were always connected, despite being thousands of miles away from each other. And that's what stories do! Stories make us laugh. Make us cry. Make us dream. Make us fly. And most importantly, they help you re-connect and re-live your best moments.

We bonded yet again for this book, with Sree donning the storyteller hat this time around. And here I am, writing this foreword for 'Keep Gliding'

- a beautiful compilation of stories that Sree & Shilpa have come up with.

What I particularly love about Keep Gliding is the way each story ends. The little reveals and the unexpected twists are what makes short stories interesting. Keep Gliding is filled with them. Shilpa's breathtaking artwork helped put captivating visuals to each of these narratives.

While these stories could literally be around anything under the sun, I was particularly impressed by their attempt to use this work to raise awareness about the causes that impact the future generations. And you can feel the concern he has towards these challenges as you glide past the stories.

So, when he approached me with this opportunity to write the foreword of the book and after reading the manuscript, I felt it's my responsibility as the well-being father of a naughty 4-year-old to share the beautiful messages the creators want to convey.

I also want to congratulate you on doing your bit by picking up a copy of this book. By doing so, you have contributed to keeping alive the believe in future generations that the world is their oyster. As you may be aware, all royalties will be passed onto UNICEF to support children's development.

To round off, I wish Keep Gliding all the success and may this just be the start for its creators.

Sandeep Balan

(A branded content pioneer and writer, Sandeep's stories have had over 500 million views on the internet)

Table of Contents

Self-Made

And the winner of the CEO of the year award is….
Michaelll Jooseph.

Michael Joseph, that's me. I was not surprised. If anything, I would have been surprised had I not won. I stood up to walk towards the stage and silently replayed my acceptance speech one more time.

'I have worked hard for this. And I truly believe that I completely deserve this.

This award is testimony to my resilience and undying determination which has seen me through every challenge that life has thrown at me.

As I stand before you, I want to share my success mantra. Success is a product of your and only your hard work. Never rely on another set of shoulders to achieve anything you aspire for.

All the very best to you all.'

As I walked up the stairs towards the podium, my feet caught each other and sent me rolling down. Darkness and silence instantly set in. It was followed by a small light that got bigger and bigger. Shades of greenery started to appear. Rectangular figures started forming. A big gate emerged which I instantly recognised as that of my school. Next to the gate, I could see my father speaking to the school watchman whose name I could not recollect.

My father was sweating, and I got closer to listen in. He was telling the watchman about missing the deadline for my admission application submission by ten minutes. His eyes got wet as he shared how big a setback this was for me and the family. The watchman asked if he had tried speaking to the headteacher, to which he replied in the negative. 'She comes out in 15 mins. Why don't you try speaking to her?' were the next words of the watchman. My attention moved to the diary that my father was holding. It mentioned 1986, my first school year.

Darkness took over before paving way to the image of a young me reading a letter. I recognised that moment immediately. After 3 failed attempts to get into the University of my dreams, I had finally got through. I was extremely proud of myself. Attention zoomed in to the contents of the letter which congratulated me while adding that another candidate had backed out which opened the place I was being offered.

The letter split into small pieces that transformed into my first boardroom meeting. I was pitching my brilliant idea that the board were less excited about. I was vehemently defending it. Arguments were going back and forth, and personal pride of the members was taking over objectivity. The doorbell rang and in came a waiter who served tea, coffee and biscuits. Ironically, the hot beverages cooled the room. I then saw myself walking out with the funding approval I was after.

Bright light now started surrounding me. A voice asked if I was okay to which I indicated in the affirmative. I was back on my feet and proceeded to the stage. After accepting the award, I delivered my acceptance speech.

'I have worked hard for this. And I truly believe that I completely deserve this.

But this is not the fruit of my efforts alone. Many have knowingly or unknowingly lent their shoulders or helped me get up when I have fallen.

While this award acknowledges my resilience and undying determination, it is testimony that success is never down to individual effort alone. It involves choices others make for you. It involves working with and for each other. Above all, it involves interventions beyond your control.

When I look at this award, I will be reminded of every fall I have had. I will also be reminded that the dots join when you look back and not forward. May you all be able to do so as well.

Thank you very much and all the very best.'

Hole in the Wall

'We shall overcome. We shall overcome. We shall overcome someday...'

The group sang even as one more among them became silent. But no-one could afford to tend to the fading voices. This was a life rule that had already been wired into them.

One part of them kept moving up and another in the opposite direction. The thick dry cold soil through which they were moving made it seem an impossible mission. Their water resources had exhausted. The pace of progression was slowing with each moment. The prayers from inside for a few drops of water was intensifying.

'We will walk hand in hand. We will walk hand in hand.

We do believe deep in our hearts. We shall overcome someday…'

The last line was barely completed than six more hands let go. More than the reduced numbers, the group noticed the change around them. They noticed the moisture level increasing and the cold starting to give way to warmth. They thought their prayers were getting answered.

A few drops of water touched them. Fresh energy started to spread like a bushfire among them. We must be near, they believed. The prayers were replaced for a moment with gratitude to the energies.

That replacement was short lived. Maybe the energies prefer prayers to gratitude. The water drops became unrecognisable. They came down with the greatest force the group had encountered. One of them went...

'We are not afraid. We are not afraid.

We are not afraid today...'

The others joined in. The force of the water kept increasing as if adamant to break the group's spirit. More and more voices faded away. The water pushed them back almost till halfway of the distance they had travelled. The floodgates from the skies then decided to close. The unit strength had been reduced to seven.

'We shall all be free. We shall all be free.

We shall all be free someday….'

The flood might have reduced their numbers, but it could not dent their spirit. The water brought their physical and mental strengths at par. They kept marching at the fastest pace they had done. They passed the remains of the landmarks they had seen before and were soon surrounded by new ones.

The warmth started to increase. They saw beams of sunlight seeping through. Some of the sun's rays were almost touching their bodies. They got to the walls that stood between them and the world they had been longing to reach.

Each of them made a hole in the wall and got through. For the first time, they felt what it was like to be above the ground. And that was mission accomplished. And that was hope kept alive for more generations.

Celebration was in order and they did in the way the entire unit had planned at the start. By looking towards the sun, the blooming flowers danced along, swaying their stems and humming the lines they had kept for this moment.

'We have overcome. We have overcome.

We have overcome today.

We have kept hope alive. We have kept hope alive.

We have kept hope alive for tomorrow.'

Keep Gliding

'You ready girl?'

'Yes Mamma'

'Let's go then.'

Ever since Eva could remember, she had dreamt of her maiden trip to the south. The trip was an annual ritual for Eva's clan to escape the dropping temperatures.

Mamma had told her many stories of the beautiful sights on the way. Counting the camels on the Sahara, spotting the king of the jungle, the night sky over the Indian Ocean and the biggest prize of them all – the largest mammal on Earth. Eva could not wait to tick these off her list.

35 days into the trip, Eva had managed to tick off all but one thing. The mighty blue whale kept eluding her.

'What's your name girl?' went a voice. Eva looked to her side and noticed the most beautiful feathers she had laid eyes on. 'Sorry. Who are you?' she asked. 'My apologies. Introductions are in order. I am Dee. I belong to the Teek family from Asia. There are 5000 of us this year. What's your name?' The Yellow mountain in the Indian Ocean had for centuries been the meeting point of the Asians and the Europeans.

'I am Eva. I fly from Europe as part of the Maple clan.'

'Well. Nice to meet you Eva'

Eva smiled.

'Is that your bucket list? First trip?' asked Dee. Eva nodded in affirmation.

'It's my third. What have you got left?'

'Blue whale' came Eva's answer.

'Oh!!! That's a tough one. I had to wait for my second trip to spot the giant.' Dee noticed Eva's shoulders drooping. To shoot up the positivity quotient, he quickly followed up with, 'Something tells me though that you will see it on your first. And something is never wrong.' Dee winked his eye as he said this. Eva cheered up immediately.

'You don't say much. Do you?' went Dee. Eva smiled again. 'You mind if I glide with you? I would like to spot the blue whale as well.' Eva smiled and off they glided together.

Three months past and Eva and Dee found themselves above Yellow mountain again. In their immediate vicinity were Sam, Rocky and Jasmin. Known as 'The Gang', the five of them had become famous among their clans for their friendship. Today though was about goodbyes for the 5 friends, at least for now.

'So this is it.' said Dee. Eva smiled, this time with a tinge less happiness than usual. 'You promise we will meet here next time?'. 'I promise' came Eva's quick reply. Dee, Jasmin, Sam and the rest of the Teek family waved goodbye and headed off towards the East. Eva, Rocky, Mamma and the Maple clan continued North.

Our planet did another half trip around the sun and it was time for Eva to make her second journey to the reefs.

'Johnny. Jacob. You ready boys?'

'Yes Mamma.'

'What are you most excited about?' asked Eva

'Ticking off everything on our bucket list' came their reply. 'What are you excited about Mamma?'

'Seeing your daddy', smiled Eva as she answered.

Eva, Johnny, Jacob and Mamma joined the rest of the Maple clan.

'Johnny look. There's an elephant.' said Jacob. 'And a giraffe.' Added Johnny. 'Tick and tick' went the two of them together as they flew across the Savanna.

Eva though saw different scenes from her last trip. More than the elephant, she saw the narrow dry river. More than the beings that moved, she saw bones of earth creatures that vultures were parched on. Her body felt warmer than she could recall from her last trip. A few feathers left her body and descended towards the river.

'Mamma. I don't recall these sights from last time. I am also feeling much warmer.' Eva shared with her mother. 'Eva my dear. The excitement of your first trip and the bucket list was the reason you did not see it last time', came Mamma's reply.

She continued, 'Each year I make this trip, I feel warmer and warmer. I see fewer and fewer signs of life. The green distribution I had seen on my first trip was 10 times the size of what you saw last year. If you look around, you will notice that the Maple clan that made the trip last year was much bigger than those with us today.' Eva looked around and noticed the wider space between her clan members than she remembered from last time.

'Why is that happening Mamma?'

'I don't know dear. All I know is that our world is changing faster than we can cope with. Next year, even fewer of us will make this trip.' Eva felt her Mamma's heavy heart from within her. She did not ask anything more.

'Mamma. Come see the king of the jungle.' Johnny called.

Eva looked at her mother. Without saying a word her mother understood the question Eva was seeking a reply for. Mamma nodded slowly. Eva smiled at her. She then smiled at the boys and told them. 'All part of the beautiful world we live in.' And they glided down to get a closer look.

****

PS: Only 100 members of the Teek family joined the trip that year. Dee was not one of them. A very different looking Jasmin (half her feathers gone and some parts of her body showing the remains of burns) told Eva about the forest fires that sent the Teek family into starvation. Eva closed her eyes as a tear trickled down her cheek. She then put on a smile and flew towards the boys.

Magic Potion

It was bath time. And not just bath time but OIL bath time. To understand how 4-year-old Lakshmi was feeling, imagine her as a tiger. Now imagine her being fed broccoli. Now imagine her being fed carrots. Now imagine her being fed both!!!

The oil bath ritual was something that Gowri, my wife, handled. She had the charm (read as usage of spine-chilling eye-popping stares and some threats involving lack of screen time/chocolates etc) to get it done without much hue and cry. I though, possessed less of that charm. So, when I found myself in charge of oil bath today, I was starting to feel a bit like that tiger.

But there was no escaping. So, like a grown up, I decided to roll up my sleeves and transform into a brave tiger. I let out a roar (loud inside and silent outside) to get into the part. Step 1 was to get the oil. Step 2 was to heat it up. Step 3 onwards is not relevant for this narrative.

I took the bottle from the cupboard to realise that it was empty. I recollected that new supplies had arrived yesterday. I opened the carton, touched each bottle and went - January, February, March, April, May and June. Enough to last us till our next India trip.

I took one out and admiration set in for the resilience of the little bottle and its contents. While there were some signs of tiredness (the usual liquid substance was semi solid), not a single drop seemed to have got out. Even more remarkable when you think of the journey it had made.

Starting in a train from the Venice of the East (Alappuzha, Kerala) to the Oxford of the East (Pune, Maharashtra),

followed by a road trip to the City of Dreams (Mumbai)

culminating in a flight over several countries and time zones to arrive in the Festival Capital of the World (Edinburgh, Scotland)

After a few seconds of showing my respect to the little bottle, I moved on to Step 2. Turned on the hob, transferred a small portion of the oil into a pan and let the flames do their job.

As the aromas started flowing through the house, I unknowingly closed my eyes. I saw a 4-year-old me lying next to Ammamma (meaning grandmother in the language Malayalam) as she recited my favourite bedtime story – how the sons of Queen Sita stood up to their father, King Rama. I saw her beautiful, curly, black hair, that despite her age, did not have a single grey. Her fish shaped eyes and buttery cream skin still leaving me in awe.

The visuals shifted to a young me being readied for oil bath. Just like Lakshmi, at that age, I did not like the smell of oil. I would run around the house as Ammamma followed me with oil in her hand. I did this till she got tired, at which point, I would run towards her and cover her saree with oil from my body.

Recollection of the laborious oil making process followed. All the ingredients were handpicked by Achachan (my grandfather) with some seasonal ones needing sourced several months in advance. They were hand ground, mixed in the right order and at the right temperature to create what Ammamma referred to as her magic potion. She would not let any of her helpers near the process as she trusted none other than herself to guarantee the quality that her grandson deserves.

The next breath of the fragrance transported me to my later years, when I was thousands of kilometers away from Ammamma. Oil baths and her magic potion though, continued to be a part of me. This time, more by choice than force. It was amazing how fresh supply always arrived before my stock ran out. That was until they completely stopped arriving.

Since then, I have tried other oils available in the market. But they were not even close to Ammamma's magic potion – neither the smell nor the feel. Perhaps Lakshmi, my grandmother, was not making up the part about the magic.

I opened my eyes and a few tears trickled down. The oil in the pan was ready, filling the entire house with its aroma. As for me, I had finally discovered what the magic ingredient was.

'Ewww.. Dadda what is that yucky smell??', my daughter Lakshmi shouted from upstairs. I smiled and replied. 'It's the smell of love my dear. The smell of love.' And the circle of magic continued...

Strawberry Fields Forever

'Sajeev, is the car ready?'

'Yes Madam'

'Sandhya, has someone gone to pick the ornaments?'

'Yes Aunty'

'Suresh, what's happening with the catering person?'

'He has reached the site Madam.'

'Mamma, mamma'

'Yes Sama'

'Relax. It's all in hand.'

I turned my head towards Sajeev. 'Mamma. Look at me. Look at me!' I did and she looked me in the eye and said calmly. 'It's all in hand. Trust me it is.'

I sat down and Sama gave me a tight squeeze. I needed it. For a moment, I was able to do what she asked me to. The tiny face that had relieved me of 40 hours of brutal pain was all I saw. And here she was, getting ready to share her life with another beautiful soul.

As the doorbell rang I called out, 'Sajeev, can't you hear the doorbell ringing?' No reply. 'Sajeev, where are you?' While I briskly proceeded to the house door, I caught a glimpse of Sama shaking her head and shrugging her shoulders, indicating to me that I will never change. I opened the door with a smile.

Only for it to be wiped off immediately at the sight of the man standing in front.

I felt raindrops on my face. They were hitting me as if stones were being pelted on me. I was walking in a thunderstorm surrounded by hills and greenery as tears rolled profusely down my cheeks.

'Are you okay?' A stranger asked me. Even the heavy rain could not camouflage my feelings from the world. He asked again 'Are you okay? Can I help you?'. I replied, 'I am looking to find the way to town'.

'It's that way', pointing in the direction opposite to the one I was proceeding on. 'I am going that way. Would you like to come with me?' I joined him as he extended his umbrella.

As we were walking, I was transported to the Howrah Bridge in Kolkota where I was standing feeling the same way – lost and petrified. On that instance we were out on a walk to explore the city new to both of us. An argument had erupted, and his response was to overpower my voice with his. Followed by walking away, leaving me alone to find my way back.

Then flashed the image of a similar me on a frosty wintery night. This time standing in front of my house with Viswa inside me. I was ringing the doorbell at 11PM with no response till 11:30PM.

'You deserve this. What do you mean you were working till now? It's your duty, not mine, to ensure this is taken care' Along with these words he gave a few punches to the wall. The pain though was felt where it was intended, crumbling my heart.

The next day I was holding his hand as we sat together sipping coffee from my favourite mug. I told myself that no one is perfect and we have to forgive the flaws of those we love.

As if woken back by the raindrops, I heard the stranger say 'I am Brian'. Nothing he said thereafter travelled beyond my outer ear as the screams from 30 minutes back echoed inside me.

'Get out. I said get out of my car right now. When I say now, I mean NOW.' A scared me followed his command. I had barely got out as he threw my bag from the car and drove off.

'Mamma. Who is at the door?' Viswa came to me and saw the figure in front of me. 'Dad! You made it.' Viswa called out 'Sama. Dad is here.' I saw an excited Sama come running as I walked towards my room.

Sajeev came over to me and asked, 'Madam. Where do you want these flowers?' I looked at him angrily and shouted. 'Did I not tell you to hang them at the entrance?' I shook my head. He said, 'Ahh... Sorry. I am doing it straightaway.' I said, 'Wait. Did you finish labelling the tables?' 'Yes Madam'. 'Thank God. At least you got that right.' went my agitated response.

Two of the most enjoyable days of my life followed. Sama's happy and excited face was worth all the mayhem I had to content with to ensure everything was exactly how she wanted it to be. The loud sounds slowly started to fade away. Soon, it was just

Viswa and me left in the house. A stark contrast to the last few weeks.

Viswa asked, 'Mamma, do you want a coffee? I am making one for me.' I said, 'Yes please.'

I sat on my favourite chair and asked Alexa to put on the Beetles. Alexa did so, and Strawberry fields came on.

I hummed my favourite lines as the song played

'Let me take you down

'Cause I'am going to Strawberry fields

Nothing is real

And nothing to get hung about

Strawberry fields forever'

Viswa handed over my favourite mug as the Beetles continued to help us wind down. He hugged me, sat next to my chair and whispered. 'You did great Mamma. You did great.' I gave him a kiss, pulled a throw over me, closed my eyes and joined back with the Beetles.

'Living is easy with eyes closed

Misunderstanding all you see

It's getting hard to be someone

But It all works out

It doesn't matter much to me'

Memory Catchers

'Is that Jade's great grandchild?' Debbie quizzed Luke.

Unlike their peers, Debbie and Luke had always lived in the same neck of the woods. Their peers had either been forced out or had withered away with time.

'Yes' came Luke's reply while adding, 'Looks like it's her first day to school.' Debbie and Luke had spent their entire life keeping tab of the events around them. They particularly enjoyed the morning sights of the world easing into its routine. The routines itself subject to constant change.

Jade's family was of special interest to them as, like the two of them, Jade's bloodline always lived in the same woods.

'Do you remember when Jade and Sam used to visit the woods? The two were inseparable.', recalled Luke.

Debbie added, 'I also remember them warning their children to stay away from the woods. When they were saying it, I so wished that I could show their children all the things they did in the woods. It would have been a good laugh to see them justify the woods being unsafe after that.'

'In their defence though, it had only been two days since we bore witness to Serena holding a knife with blood dripping of it and Deepak lying covered in blood.' came Luke's reminder.

'Look. Jade's great grandchild has fallen out. Is she hurt?' interrupted Debbie. 'Her name is Samaara Debbie and she is fine.' mentioned a mildly annoyed Luke.

Hardly noticing Luke's annoyance, Debbie went on recalling her memories. 'This day has changed so much over the seasons. My first memory is of only boys going to school and that too only a few. Now girls go, and I can hardly count how many we see. The kids have also got happier each year.' A happier Luke added. 'I agree with the last part.'

'There comes Max, Luke.' Debbie shifted their attention towards Max, the dog while adding, 'I hope he does not choose us today.' Max was not one of Luke and Debbie's favourite. He wouldn't be yours either if he poo-ed or wee-ed on you.

Max ran in Luke and Debbie's direction while the two friends kept praying, 'Please, please, please. Not on us today.' Max's speed increased but not as fast as the anxiety level of Debbie. Max stopped in his strides and relaxed himself on the lamp post. Phew!!! Debbie and Luke had escaped on this instance.

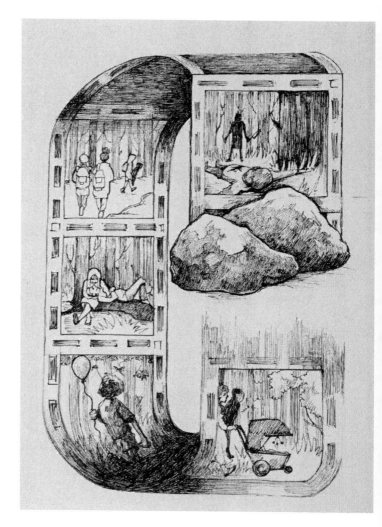

'Sometimes I wonder Luke, what fun it will be to show our memories to others. It will be a good laugh to see their reactions when they realize how little they know. And most of what they think as truth is incorrect.' A thoughtful Debbie shared.

'Debbie. Our role is to capture the memories and keep them safe. I am sure a day will come when another creature would be able to see the memories we hold. When it does, us rocks will be...'

'Hey Luke, there's baby Cheryl.' Interrupted Debbie leaving Luke annoyed. Again!!!

Open Your Eyes

'Pass the ball. I am free.' 'Jim. Cross, cross.' 'Salma, want to play with me?' 'That's a cool hockey stick Rachel.' 'He loves me, he loves me not.'

The lunch bell had rung 15 minutes ago. Despite the dark skies and naked trees, typical for this time of the year, the happiness quotient in the school was at its highest.

Salma ran happily to Eric. 'Do you want to go to our favorite part of the ground?' asked Eric. Salma nodded with her widest smile.

The usually very busy corner of the ground was devoid of any feet today. Perhaps it was the slimy mud (there had been heavy rain and lightning the night before). Or maybe it was the cold. Or maybe the lightning left a curse as Josh had told everyone in class. Whatever be the reason, the two friends didn't mind having the entire area to themselves.

Salma filled her fist with wet soil. 'Eric', she called. Eric who was walking in front turned towards her. Within milliseconds, he landed on his back. Salma's mud bomb had hit Bullseye. She laughed. Eric immediately gave Salma a taste of her own medicine.

Salma started humming the Beethoven tune they were learning in their piano class. Eric joined to give it the symphony effect. It felt like two artists were creating a painting version of Beethoven, on each other using mud.

Eric started to drain but Salma was showing no signs of slowing down. Eric said, 'I give up. You win Queen.' The rule was to address the other as King or Queen when you admit defeat. Salma stopped and commanded. 'Kneel peasant.'

Eric gathered his energy, slowly kneeled and lowered his head in front of Salma. Salma could hardly hide her giggles as she went on, 'Your Queen is very pleased to take you under her protection. You may rise peasant Eric.' Loud giggles escaped their lips.

Eric asked, 'Dear Queen. As a token of my gratitude may I build a castle in your honour?' 'That will make the Queen very happy.' came the reply. They started digging the mud. Eric turned back to grab some mud from behind him. 'Move Eric', screamed Salma.

Eric felt a salty taste in his mouth. His memory cells signaled to him that it was the same taste from when he lost his first tooth, about a week back. Unlike last week though, his jaws were paining badly.

His feet not touching anything told him that he was hanging in the air. Eric opened his eyes and saw John's face in front. 'Leave him John. Put him down.' shouted Salma.

John threw Eric down and said. 'This is my last warning to you brother. You are not to kneel before them.' He then turned around to Salma and went on. 'You little thing. Don't ever come near my brother.' 'Run Salma run.' Eric shouted. Salma looked John in his eyes and did not move. Her heart was not ready to back down. 'Salma, please listen to me.' Eric pleaded.

Her brain started to overpower her heart. Salma broke eye contact, turned around and slowly started to run. Her eyelids travelled towards each other and were joined by her palm and fingers. She rubbed her eyes and opened her eyes.

Darkness surrounded her. The only sound she could hear was tic-tic-tic-tic. She rubbed her eyes again. A circular figure started to form. It seemed like a lamp shade.

Her hands moved beside her. She felt a soft surface. She turned to her left and saw her Papa. From deep within she went, 'Papa, look at me. Papa, please look at me.' She heard the clock go tic-tic-tic.

She prayed again, 'Papa, please open your eyes.' Papa opened his eyes. She cuddled him. Papa reciprocated. 'I am scared Papa.' Salma whispered. Papa kissed her on her cheeks and whispered back. 'Don't worry Salma. I am here. Go to sleep my princess' and he patted her.

'Can you put on my lullaby?' Salma asked. Papa turned, got his phone and put on her favourite lullaby. He wrapped his arms around her and continued to pat her. The lullaby took over from the clock, both in the room and in Salma's head. Salma and Papa closed their eyes and its stayed that way even after the lullaby stopped.

School Run

Mid-August 2020

Schools have reopened. The girls were going back to school after months of being at home. Thanks to COVID restrictions.

Up until last school year, our family had relied on breakfast/after school clubs and always used the car to do school rounds. With us continuing to work from home, for the first time in my life, I could do 'school runs' and not 'school drives'. A prospect that I found very exciting.

The girls and I proceeded to school. We walked

through the woods and chit chatted all the way. The topics varied, and we played games like I spy, guess who, guess the number etc. Got to school and the girls ran to their friends, hardly even waving goodbye. I turned back and ran home thinking how great this was.

A week in

'Jenny… Come on… Quicker'. 5 mins later. 'Jenny… Catch up….' The different pace at which each of us were moving was becoming the focus of most of the journey. After their drop, I thought about what could be done differently to increase the pace.

How about introducing some metrics? After all, we behave based on how we are measured. Right? When the girls got home that day, I sat down with them and we discussed about timing our school runs. The aim being to better it each day. The two of them were quickly on board. I went 'You are a genius Mark. This will work.'

Come on girls

Day 1 – 25 minutes 24 seconds, Day 2 – 22 minutes 15 seconds, Day 3 – 21 minutes 17 seconds, Day 4 – 20 minutes 48 seconds, …..Day 10 – 17 minutes 24 seconds, Day 11 – 17 minutes 50 seconds.

You might notice that the law of diminishing marginal returns was showcasing itself in the school runs. I had to keep the motivation high and my way was to incentivise using metrics and provide motivational pep talks at regular intervals. 'Come on girls. Let's get to less than 15 mins. We can do this.' The girls kept responding till they could not.

On Day 12 they went - 'Papa we don't want to beat our time. We are sorry.' I went 'No. No. That's not acceptable. We have to keep going, At least till we get below 15 mins.' 'No Papa, we just want to play I spy or Guess who. We don't want to beat the time.'

Course Correction

My focus on the time had made me ignore the lack of enjoyment they were having of the journey. Their message though was very clear, and I could not ignore it anymore. We did not time our trip to the school that day. We just chatted and played some games.

On my way home, I walked slower than usual. I looked around a little more. I could hear the birds chirping. I saw more of the autumn colours on the trees and the ducks swimming in the river. The smell of the pony poo did not escape me (I wish it did though).

My obsession with the numbers was taking away my ability to have a rounded view of things. And more importantly, unknowingly this was denying the girls the opportunity to appreciate the beautiful world we live in. I had to course correct.

That evening, the girls and I sat down and

discussed our day. We talked through what each of us felt. I apologised and said that we should stop timing our runs. I thought this would make them happy and was what they wanted. Wrong again!!!

To my surprise, their reaction was very different. Jenny said, 'It's not that I don't like the timing. It's just that I don't like it when we do it every day.' Jessie went, 'Yes. If some days, we could just talk to you while walking that will be fun.'

And thus, was formed our current schedule. We time our runs every alternate day and we don't on the others. The emphasis was shifted from being successful to balancing success and joy.

The Result

When we came up with this schedule I thought, this would result in us taking longer to get to below 15 mins. How wrong I was. Again!!!

On days we were timing, motivation was higher, and the kid's bodies were responding much better. Within a couple of weeks, we were consistently clocking less than 15 minutes. It was a mighty proud feeling when we did it the first time!!!

But we are not obsessed about it and have managed to count ducks, feed them sometimes, play I spy, discuss the girl fights at school (wish I had less of that to content with) and much more.

Homebound

The wheels were screaking more and more as the train got slower and slower. Sounds of the street vendors and announcements of train schedules started taking over from the wheels. The familiar smells confirmed to my brain that home was near.

I gathered my bag and joined the long queue of eager passengers looking to get off. The train halting was immediately followed by the familiar battle between the getting in and getting out team. I was glad that the getting out team got off to a good start and they maintained this position till the end.

I rushed out of the station and took the next taxi. Holding my children in my arms and seeing the delight on my wife's face kept flashing in front of my eyes. It had been over a month that the raw material sourcing for my new venture took me to the forests of Assam. I had made no contact with anyone at home in the last 2 weeks.

I rang the bell and my sister opened the door. I was surprised to see her there. My boys flung into my arms as delighted to see me as I was to see them. My wife came running with watery eyes. I hugged her and felt her transferring all her energy to the floor through me.

I called out, 'Amma (meaning mother in the language Malayalam), I am home'. There was no answer. My sister held my arm and took me to her room. Her room was uncannily clean. I called again, 'Amma, I am home'. My heart started to sink.

'Amma, I am home'. This time louder. My sister handed over her diary and said, 'Amma wanted you to have this'. I sank and lay down quietly on her bed holding her diary as tightly I could.

Why did no one inform me? Did my sister play a part in this? She must have, like she has done all through my life.

'Peacefully'. 'She went peacefully'. I slowly recognised the warmth of a very familiar grip from behind me. Sanju was holding me and whispering to me.

I felt very low about myself. Ashamed that my grief had taken me down a path of kindling the anger I had towards my sister than trying to find out what happened to Amma. 'She went to sleep and did not wake up on the morning of the 24th. It was another attack.', said Sanju.

In a feeble voice, I asked, 'Where is the note Amma wanted us to open?'. After her first heart attack, Amma had written a note for us read immediately after she goes silent forever. Sanju handed the note to me.

The note read

Smile my children. For that is the life I have lived

A life of laughs

A life of care

A life of courage

And above all, A life of adventure

Don't mock that life by making me a showpiece

Let my body feed the cycle of creation at the earliest

Let my next adventure start in the same spirit as the one I am leaving

Smile my children. For that is the life I have lived

Amma.

Angel from the War

'Don't leave me mummy and daddy', I cried loudly without anyone hearing or seeing. The school bell overpowered the cacophony of children and parents rushing off in opposite directions. But that was not why my pain was unnoticed.

I was the eldest of three children. Each new addition to the family kept cementing my belief that my younger siblings' needs were more important than mine. To cope with this, I sought 'His' help. And help 'He' did, by giving me a superpower that made my feelings invisible to the world.

The year was 1990 and this was my second school in primary one. Daddy's work used to take us to new houses and schools. New starts were never easy on me and here I was doing it again. I told myself that I have done this before, and I can do it again.

The teacher said, 'Jacob. Take the seat on the third bench.' I obeyed and kept my bag under the desk. She continued, 'Everyone take out your book and pencil.' I pulled my bag out and opened my pencil box. There was no pencil in it. I felt a hundred arrows piercing me. I could not move. I could not think. A few of the million tears stuck inside me started to slowly blur my vision.

'Take mine' said a voice from my right. When I turned, my already blurry eyes got blinded by a shining bright light. A figure with a halo started to fade in. I noticed birds flying around the halo. I thought I had reached heaven.

I wiped my eyes and the light, halo and birds faded away. The most beautiful face I had seen filled my eyes. Even without the halo, birds and light, she looked like an angel. I saw her smile and I smiled back. I took the pencil she moved towards me, said thanks and asked her, 'Are you an angel?'. She said, 'Yes. My name is Angel.' My day was made.

From then on, Angel became the single reason for me to look forward to school. We sat on the same bench. We had lunch together. We learned together. We had each other's back. We had become inseparable in the four walls where we spent most of our day. I told her everything. She would though mostly stay quiet and listen. I was convinced that she really was my angel. Life for me seemed nothing short of wonderful.

Then one day, she did not come to school. One day became two, three, four and turned into weeks and months. A fortnight after that 'one day', I overheard my teacher say that Angel must have gone back to Kuwait. 1990-1991 was when the Gulf war was going on and many families that were based in Kuwait had to return to their motherland. Angel's family was one of them. The war had ended and while that was happy news for most people, it left me devastated.

I cried silently in my bed that night. Why did she not tell me this? Why was she silent most of the time? Will I ever see her again? Why does 'He' do this to me? I cried till I had no more tears that could roll down. I dozed off when I was too tired to keep my eyes open. The next morning my experienced defence mechanism of putting on the mask took charge. I got back to living my life the way I did before meeting Angel.

Fast forward twenty years and I am living a very happy life. I share a fantastic relationship with my parents and siblings. I have the job that gets the best out of me. In Emma, I have the best companion I could have asked for. Life could not be any better.

Angel though still lurks within me. What is it that I felt for her? Was she my first true love or a great friend or a pair of ears that had time for me or one of 'His' angels or something else? Why was she very silent? These questions continue to linger but the thought of Angel only brings a smile on my face. For that very reason, I am not searching for answers.

Emma tells me that Angel is the dream whose beauty could cease if it becomes reality. I smile and work on believing that she is right.

About the Creators

Sreedev

Daughters superman Dad...
Storyteller...
Travel and nature lover...
UK based with Indian roots...
Management Professional...

Shilpa

Dreamer and mind wanderer...
Film maker...
Passionate art lover...
Strong believer in social justice
and equality among all...
National Institute of Design
Alumni...

Enjoyed our work? Reading your review will mean a lot to us. Look up for Keep Gliding on Amazon and @keepglidingthebook on Facebook and Instagram. Thanks in advance.

Printed in Great Britain
by Amazon